Volcanoes

Text: Sharon Dalgleish

Consultant: Richard Whitaker, Senior Meteorologist,

Bureau of Meteorology, Sydney, Australia

This edition first published 2003 by

MASON CREST PUBLISHERS INC.

370 Reed Road

Broomall, PA 19008

© Weldon Owen Inc.

Conceived and produced by

Weldon Owen Pty Limited

Library of Congress Cataloging-in-Publication Data

on file at the Library of Congress

ISBN: 1-59084-185-9

Printed in Singapore.

1 2 3 4 5 6 7 8 9 06 05 04 03

CONTENTS

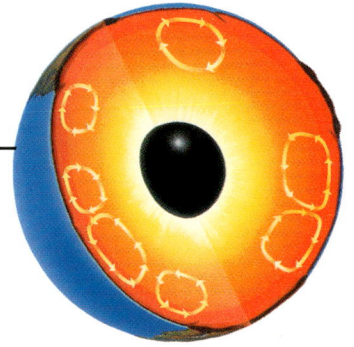

THE UNSTABLE EARTH

The outer section of the Earth is made up of jagged slabs called plates that fit together a bit like a jigsaw puzzle. Though you can't feel it, the plates are always moving. Where two plates meet, one plate sinks under the other, mixing with the hot rock below and melting to form magma. This magma pushes up to erupt as a volcano.

Ocean to Land
When a plate with thin ocean crust meets one with thick land crust, magma forms a line of volcanoes.

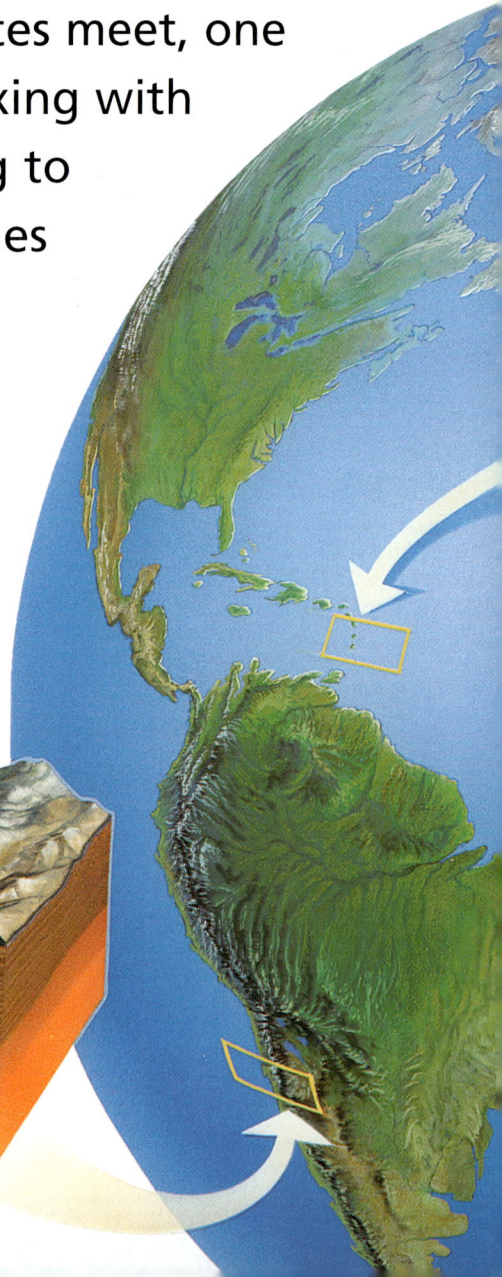

Ocean to Ocean

When the plates moving toward each other both have thin ocean crust, magma forms a chain of island volcanoes.

Land to Land

Mountains are formed when both plates have thick land crust.

MOVING PLATES

Most volcanoes and earthquakes occur along the edges of plates, where the plates meet. Countries in the center of plates, such as Australia, have few volcanoes. Countries at the edges of plates, such as Japan, have many. The map shows the directions in which the plates are moving.

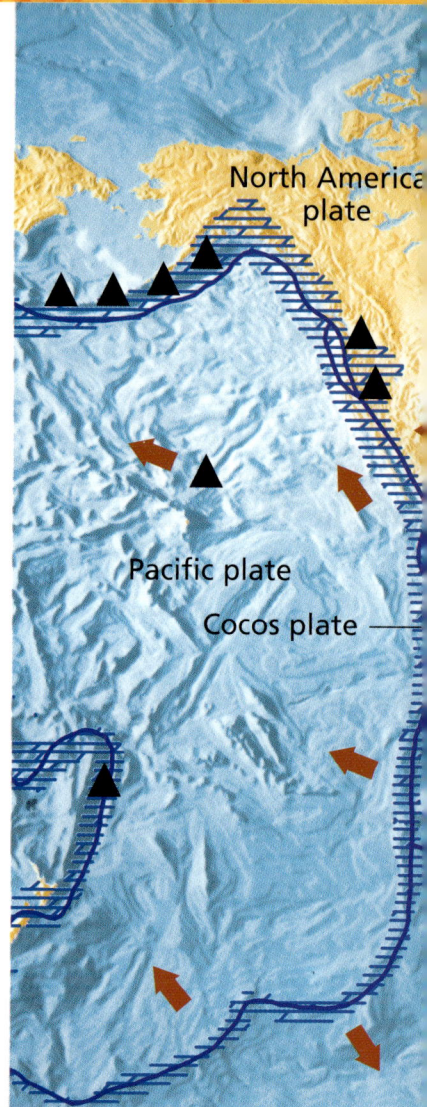

North America plate

Pacific plate

Cocos plate

Inside the Earth

The center of the Earth is a very hot, solid iron core. The arrows in the diagram on the right show how currents of heat force the plates in different directions. The surface plates float on melted rock called magma.

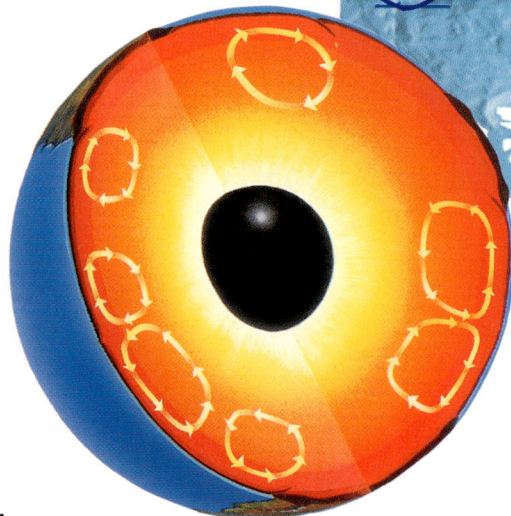

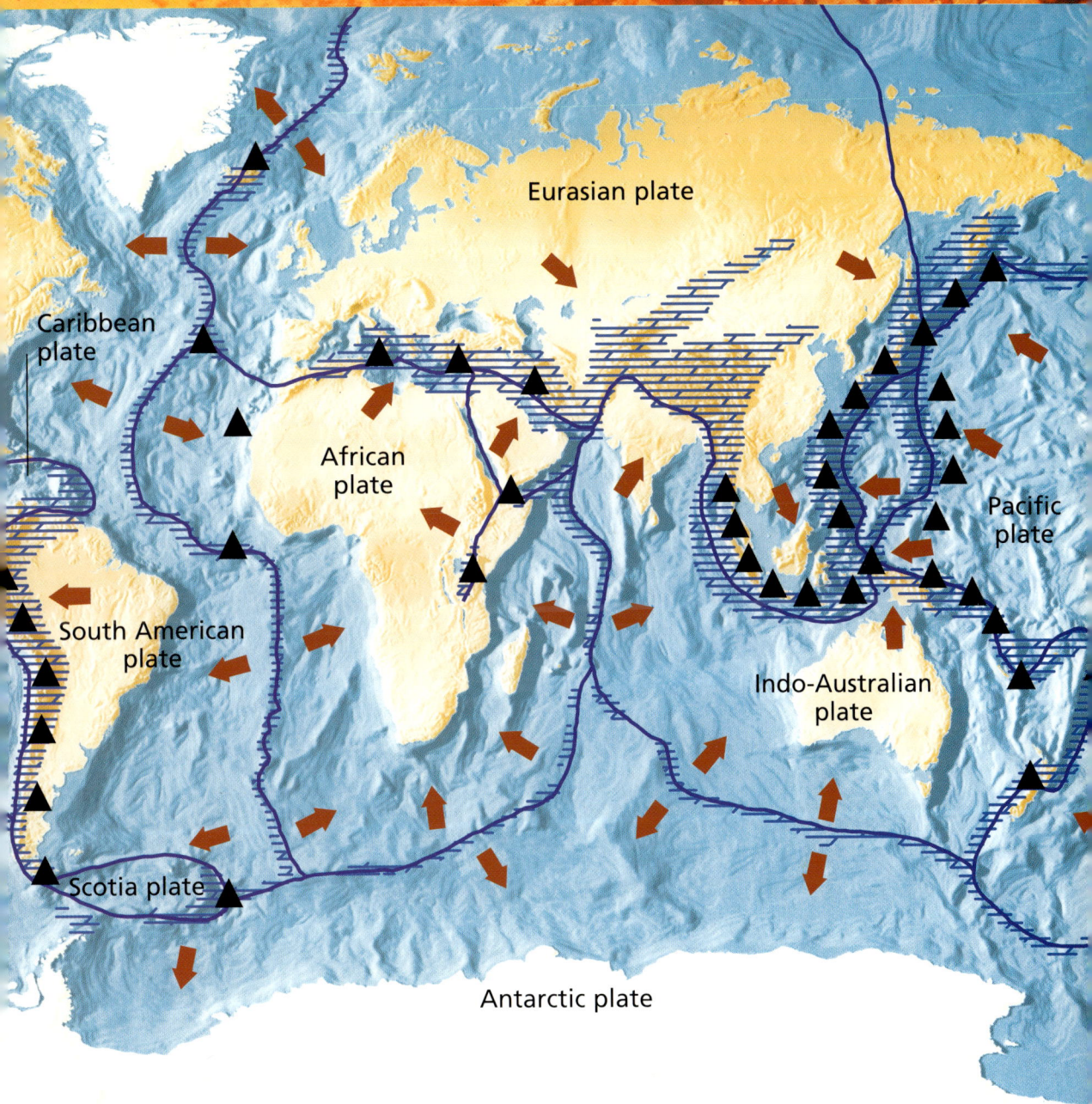

Eurasian plate

Caribbean plate

African plate

South American plate

Scotia plate

Pacific plate

Indo-Australian plate

Antarctic plate

direction of movement

▲ volcanoes

earthquake zones

Marking the Spot
This map shows
where most of the
world's hot spots are.

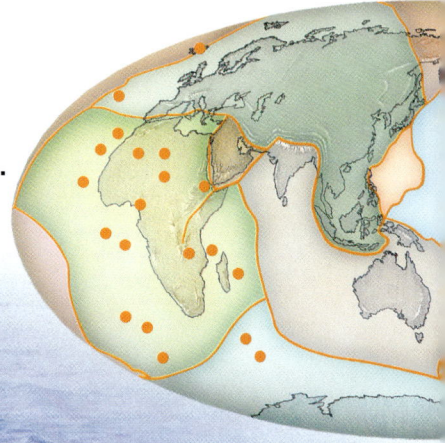

HOT SPOTS

Hot-spot volcanoes form in the middle of plates, right above a source of magma. Melted rock rises to the surface and, like a blowtorch, makes a hole in the plate. The lava then bursts through the crust. A hot spot stays still, but the plate keeps moving. Over millions of years, a string of active volcanoes become cold or dormant as they move off the hot spot.

A hot-spot volcano can erupt in a lava flow, or in a spectacular fountain like this one at Hawaii's Kilauea. Don't try to race the lava from a hot-spot volcano—it can move at speeds of 62 miles (100 kilometers) per hour!

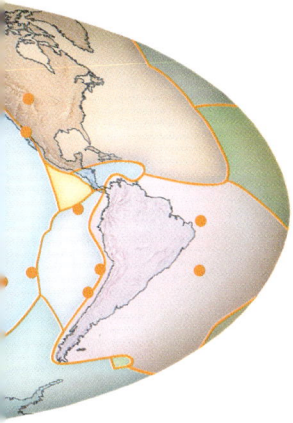

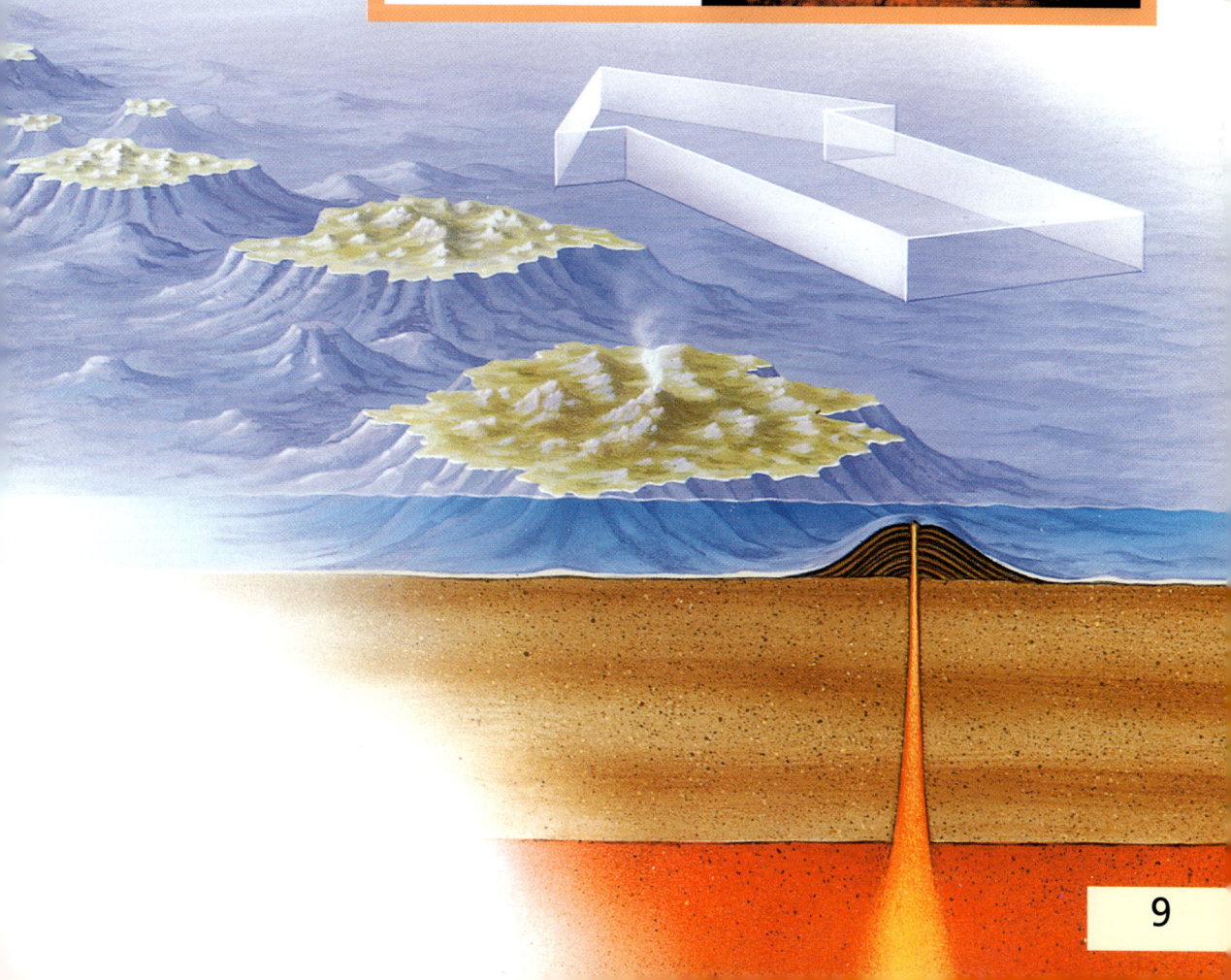

THE INSIDE STORY

small, sticky
lava bombs

large lava
bombs

cinders, gas,
and ash

Deep inside the Earth, magma rises. It gathers in pools and pushes toward the surface. If it finds a crack, it erupts as a volcano. Pieces of rock and lava blow out as volcanic ash and cinder. Steam and gas form clouds of white smoke. Small, hard bombs of lava shoot out. The magma escapes and races down the sides of the cone as a river of red-hot lava.

thin,
runny lava

thick,
sticky lava

Thick or Thin Lava
Not all eruptions are the same. The type of eruption depends on the thickness of the lava.

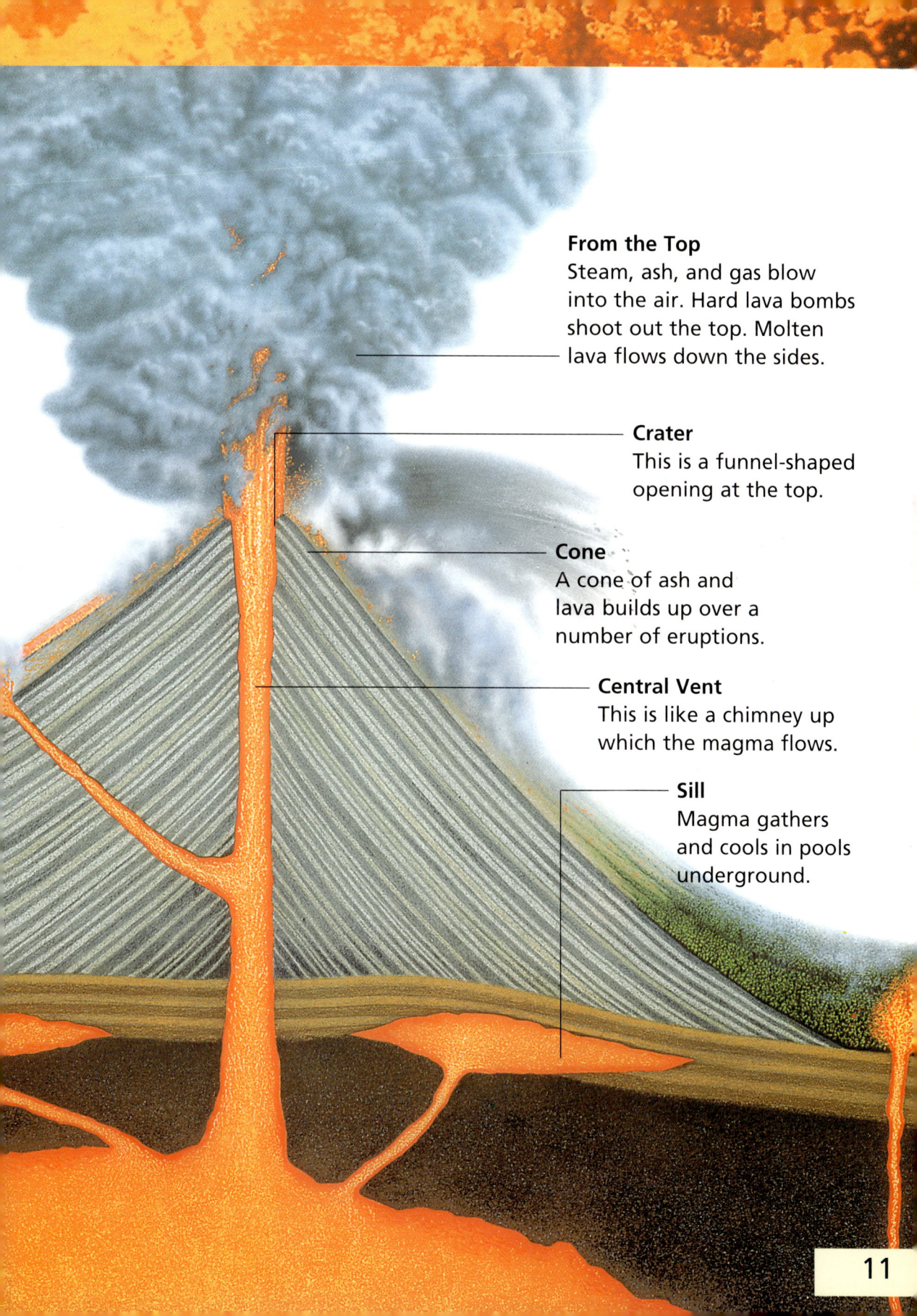

From the Top
Steam, ash, and gas blow
into the air. Hard lava bombs
shoot out the top. Molten
lava flows down the sides.

Crater
This is a funnel-shaped
opening at the top.

Cone
A cone of ash and
lava builds up over a
number of eruptions.

Central Vent
This is like a chimney up
which the magma flows.

Sill
Magma gathers
and cools in pools
underground.

Rivers of lava burn or bury any buildings in their path. Lava flows can destroy large areas of forest and farmland. Volcanoes can also collapse in on themselves, causing giant waves or avalanches. They can cause rushing mudflows more powerful than a river of water. Active volcanoes are those that might erupt at any time. Dormant volcanoes are less likely to erupt, but are waiting to erupt again. Extinct volcanoes are asleep—but don't be fooled. They sometimes wake up again!

Mountains of Fire
Lava looks spectacular, but explosions of gas, ash, and rock can be even more dangerous.

Make an Erupting Volcano

1 Use moist soil to form a mountain on a tray. Scoop out the top and put in a small dish or the lid from a spray can for a crater.

2 Pour ¼ cup of warm water into the crater. Stir in 1 tablespoon of baking soda, a few drops of red food coloring, and a few drops of liquid soap. Now pour in ¼ cup of vinegar—and watch your volcano erupt!

Step one

Step two

AMAZING!

When the island volcano of Krakatau in Indonesia erupted in 1883, the boom from the explosion was heard nearly 3,000 miles (4,800 kilometers) away.

Pyroclastic Flow
Small rocks fly into the air, while an avalanche of larger bombs the size of boulders bounces down the side of the volcano.

Ash Damage
The ash cone in this picture has blocked a road.

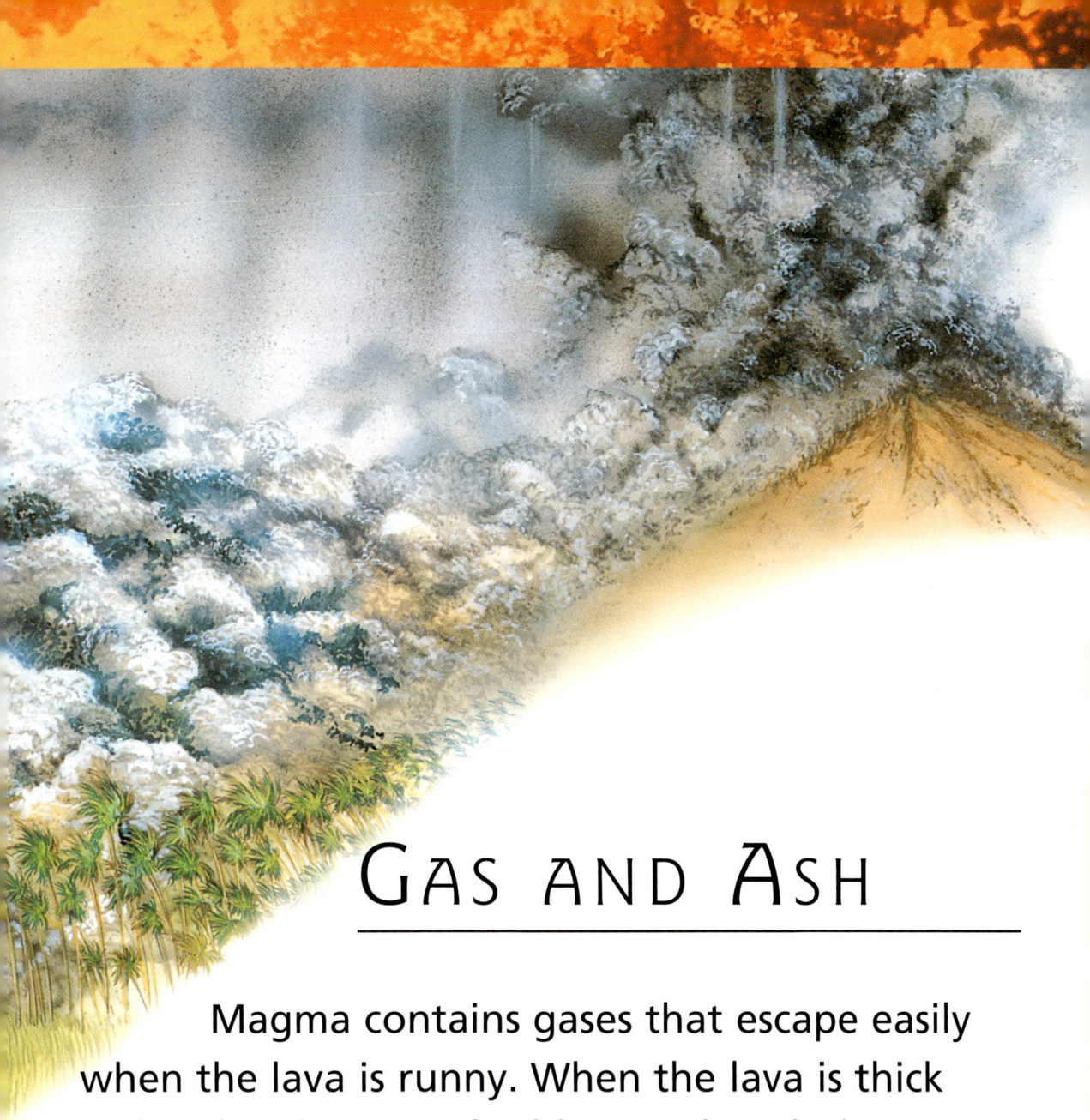

Gas and Ash

Magma contains gases that escape easily when the lava is runny. When the lava is thick and sticky, the gases build up and explode violently, flinging clouds of rock into the air. Explosions blow apart the rock and lava, creating ash. Gases and hot ash can reach speeds of 155 miles (250 kilometers) per hour.

AFTER THE ERUPTION

Volcanic eruptions cause changes to the environment. Near the volcano, there could be strong winds, rain, and mudflows for months. Clouds of fine ash can make breathing difficult. The engines of airplanes flying in the area can become clogged with dust and ash. Clouds of gases can reflect the Sun's rays back into space, causing the Earth to cool and changing our weather.

Worldwide Effect

A volcano can shoot huge amounts of ash, gas, and dust into the upper levels of the atmosphere. Strong winds carry these clouds to all parts of the world.

Volcanic Winter

Long, cold winters caused by volcanic eruptions can kill plants and crops.

Nevado del Ruiz   Armero

Mudflow
In Colombia in 1985, a 44-yard (40-m) wall of mud and ash (shown in red) flowed for 31 miles (50 km) from Nevado del Ruiz. It killed more than 23,000 people.

RIVERS OF MUD

After an eruption, ash sometimes mixes with water from melting ice or rain. This makes a thick mud, like wet cement, which flows downhill gathering stones, boulders, tree trunks—and speed. These mudflows, called "lahars," can destroy a village and kill thousands of people in minutes.

Stopping the Flow
Steel and concrete slit dams built around active volcanoes slow down mudflows so people have time to escape.

1. When a Caldera Forms
During a huge explosion, magma rises up and out the main vent.

2. Release Valve
Any magma left behind sinks back to the top of the magma chamber.

CRATERS AND CALDERAS

Craters are funnel-shaped hollows at the openings or vents of volcanoes. Very large craters called calderas are formed when normal-sized craters collapse upon themselves. Smaller eruptions can occur on the caldera floor. The world's largest caldera, at Aso in Japan, is 15 miles (24 kilometers) long and 10 miles (16 kilometers) wide. In Bali, people live in villages inside the caldera of an extinct volcano!

Crater Lakes

Lakes form when the vents of dormant or extinct volcanoes are plugged with hardened lava. Over many years, the crater fills with water from rain or snow.

4. The Collapse
Once the magma support is gone, the top collapses in on itself.

3. Empty Space
The magma then sinks below the roof of the magma chamber, where it once supported the roof.

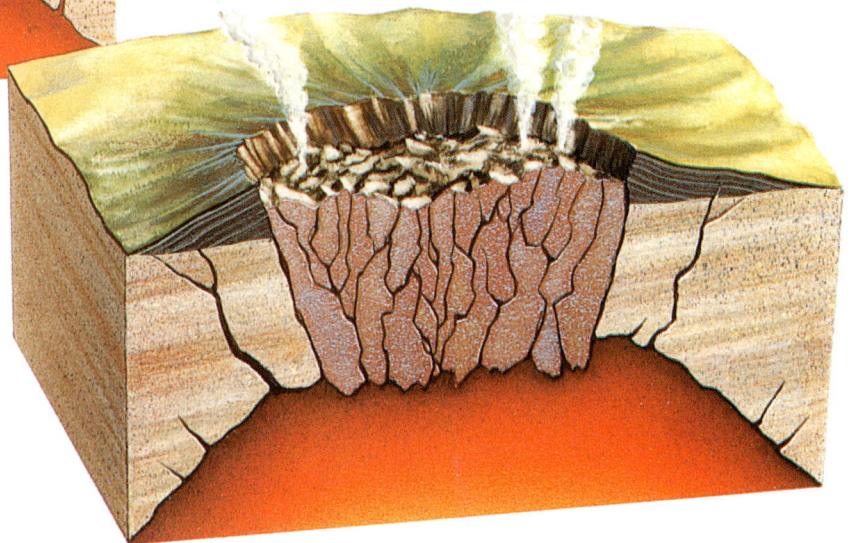

VOLCANIC LANDFORMS

Hot, molten magma rises through cracks in the Earth's surface, cooling and hardening to form rocks. Sometimes lava mixes with ash and gas, and flows downhill burying huge areas of the countryside. When wind and rain erode this volcanic rock, it can leave amazing landscapes such as these rock cones in Turkey.

Volcanic Plug
This plug in Algeria started as magma in the vent of a volcano. Over millions of years, the magma cooled and hardened. The softer rocks eroded, leaving just the plug.

Volcanic activity causes hot geysers and pools of boiling mud in Wyoming's Yellowstone National Park.

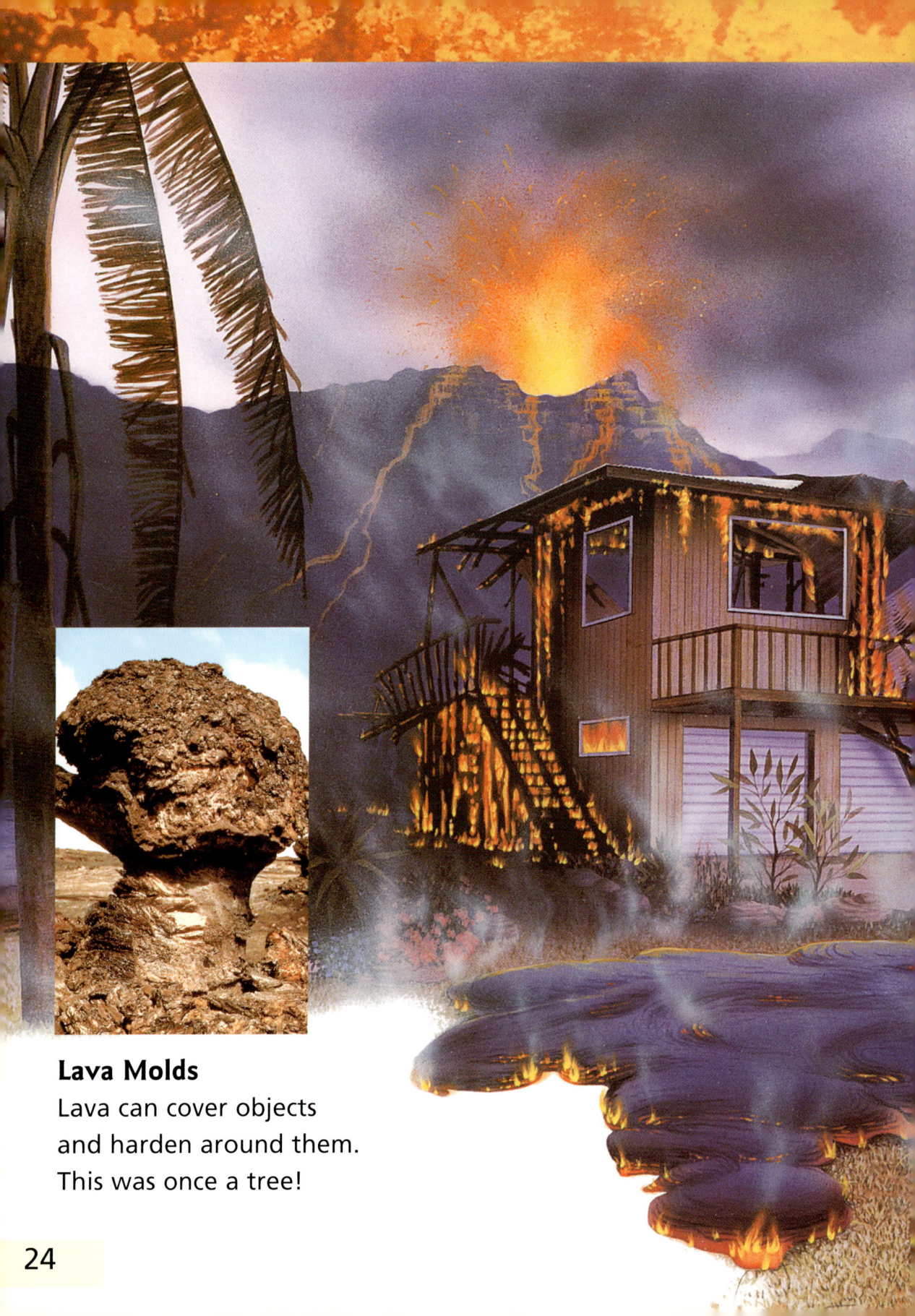

Lava Molds

Lava can cover objects
and harden around them.
This was once a tree!

Lava Flows

Lava is red-hot magma that erupts at the Earth's surface. A river of runny lava—which can be as hot as 2,192 degrees Fahrenheit (1,200 degrees Celsius)—gushes downhill from a crater or oozes from a crack in the ground. The lava stream burns everything in its path. When it cools, it adds a new layer of volcanic rock to the ground.

Tubes of Lava

If a stream of lava flows steadily for a long time, its outside may cool and form a crust. Inside the crust, the hot lava continues to flow. This forms a tube or tunnel inside. When the lava finishes flowing, the tube remains.

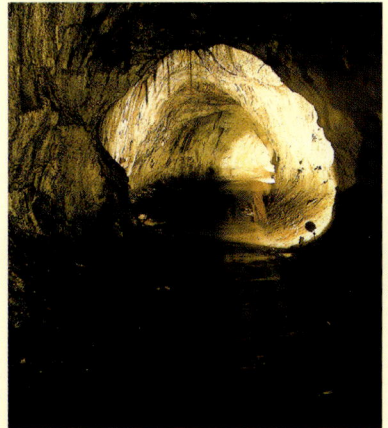

Raining Ash

Some people tried to escape the town of Herculaneum in boats. Many died when hot ash and gas covered the town.

FAMOUS VOLCANOES

Nearly 2,000 years ago, the Roman towns of Pompeii, Herculaneum, and Stabiae were destroyed when Mt. Vesuvius erupted. The people who lived nearby hadn't even realized the mountain was a volcano! Since then, Vesuvius has erupted many times. The last eruption was in 1944, and no one knows when it will erupt again. The largest active volcano in Europe is Mt. Etna. It is still active after 2,500 years of periodic eruptions.

A Volcano in the Backyard
In 1973, a seaport town in Iceland became the site of a new volcano called Eldfell.

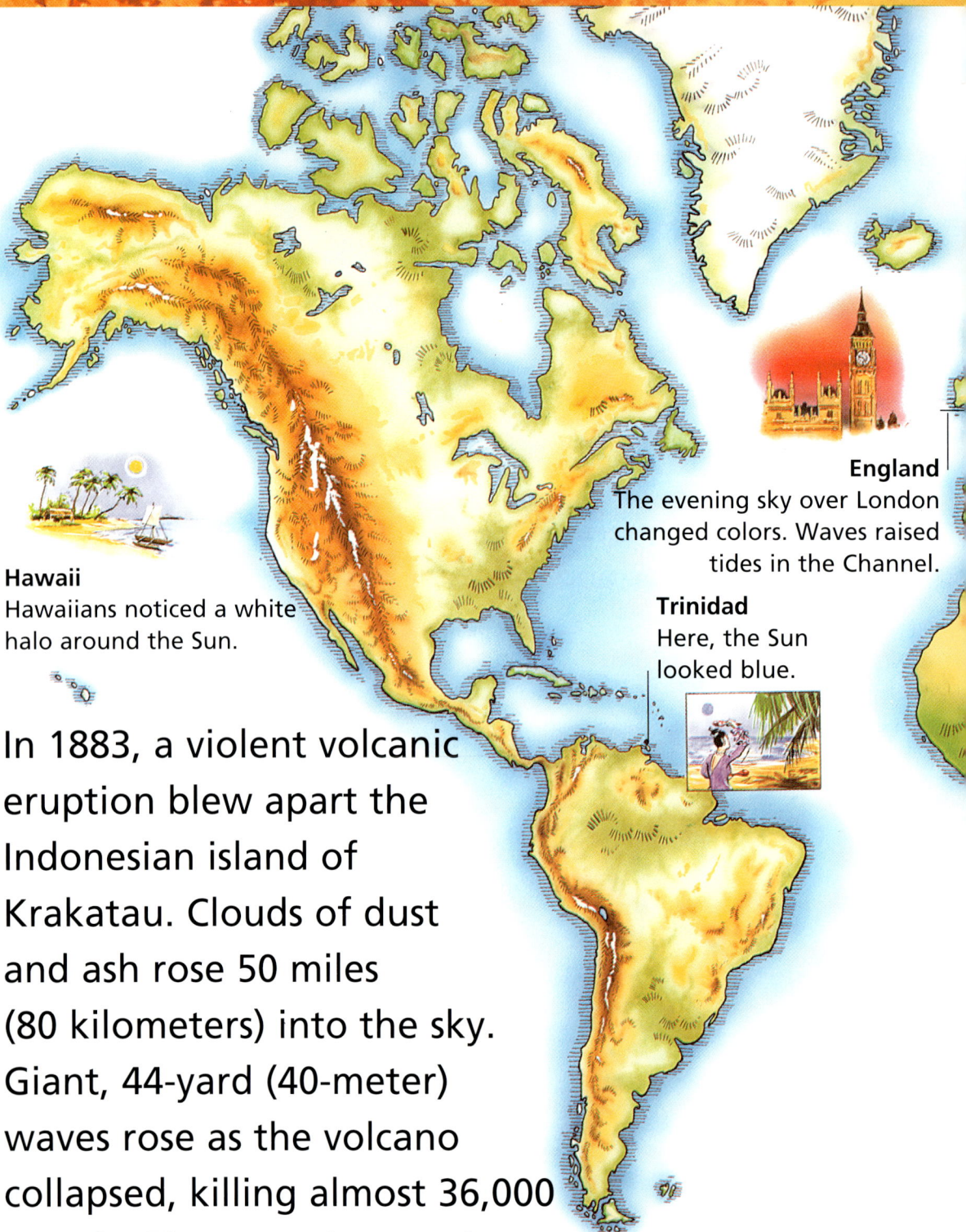

Hawaii
Hawaiians noticed a white halo around the Sun.

England
The evening sky over London changed colors. Waves raised tides in the Channel.

Trinidad
Here, the Sun looked blue.

In 1883, a violent volcanic eruption blew apart the Indonesian island of Krakatau. Clouds of dust and ash rose 50 miles (80 kilometers) into the sky. Giant, 44-yard (40-meter) waves rose as the volcano collapsed, killing almost 36,000 people. The map shows what happened around the world.

28

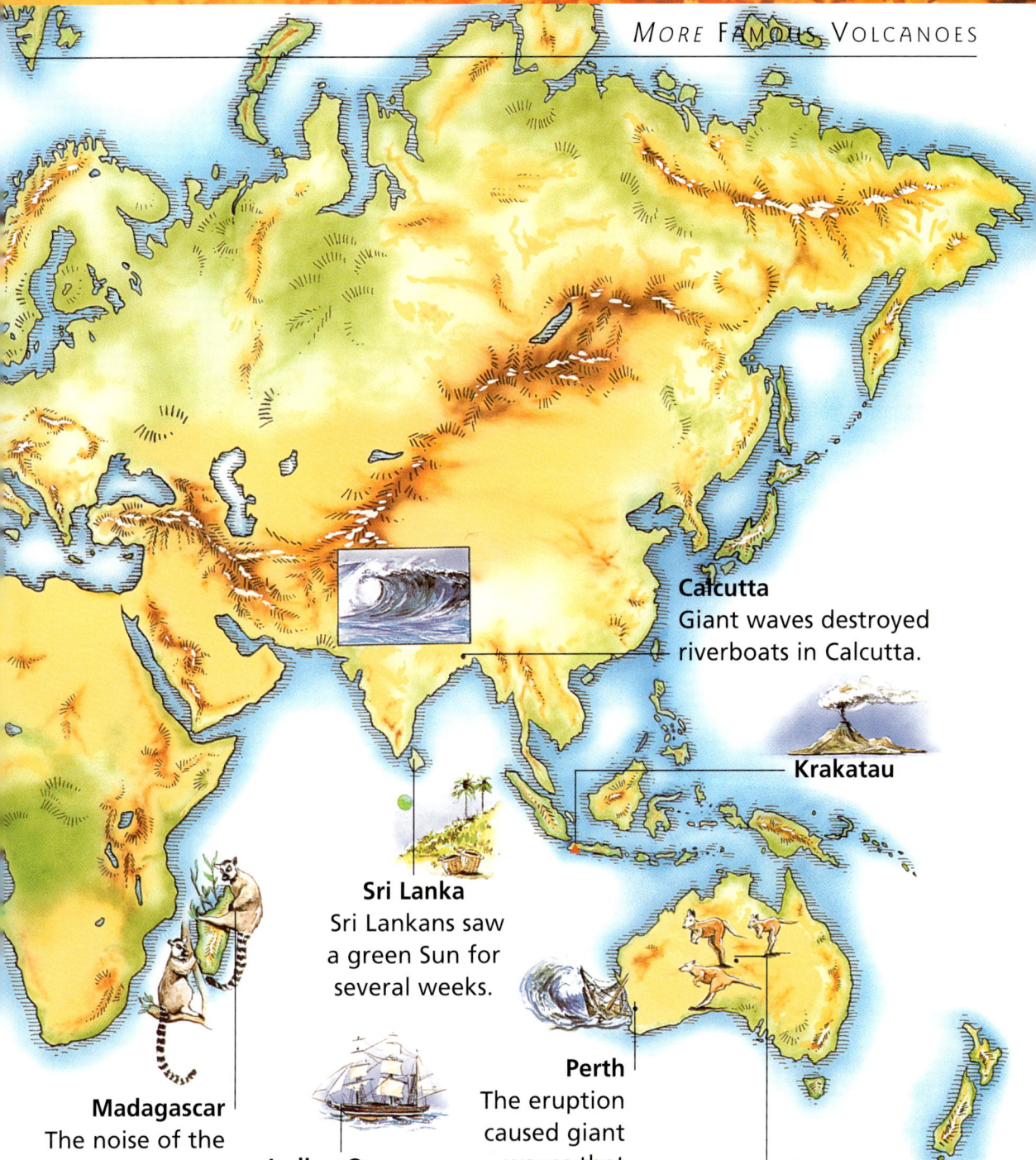

Calcutta
Giant waves destroyed riverboats in Calcutta.

Krakatau

Sri Lanka
Sri Lankans saw a green Sun for several weeks.

Madagascar
The noise of the eruption was heard as far away as Madagascar.

Indian Ocean
Up to a year later, floating rocks from the eruption blocked shipping lanes.

Perth
The eruption caused giant waves that destroyed the harbor area.

Alice Springs
The eruption sounded like rifle shots to people living here.

29

GLOSSARY

active volcano A volcano that can erupt at any time.

atmosphere The thin layer of gases that surrounds planets such as the Earth.

crust The outer layer of the Earth.

dormant volcano A volcano that is not active, but could erupt again.

erode To wear away parts of the Earth's crust to make landforms.

extinct volcano A volcano that can still erupt again, although it is highly unlikely.

geyser A hot spring that boils and erupts hot water and steam.

lava Super-heated, liquid rock that flows up through the Earth's crust and out of volcanic vents.

magma Molten rock inside the Earth.

pyroclastic flow A quickly flowing cloud of hot gas and ash blown out of the crater of a volcano.

INDEX

PICTURE AND ILLUSTRATION CREDITS

BOOKS IN THIS SERIES